Alan Haughton

Rhythm&Rag
for B flat Saxophone

Contents

1. Prelude *2*
2. Flying High *3*
3. Slow Motion *3*
4. Three's Company *4*
5. Nocturne *4*
6. Blues 9 *5*
7. Fives *5*
8. Valse – Barcarolle *6*
9. Cakewalk *6*
10. Recitative *7*
11. Iberia *8*
12. Monkey Nuts *9*
13. Cabana *10*
14. Green Tomatoes *10*
15. On Time *11*
16. Rag-a-muffin *12*

www.musicshopuk.co.uk

The Associated Board of
the Royal Schools of Music

for Stephen Davies

Rhythm & Rag for B flat Saxophone

SAXOPHONE in B♭

ALAN HAUGHTON

1. Prelude

AB 2752

2. Flying High

3. Slow Motion

4. Three's Company

5. Nocturne

6. Blues 9

7. Fives

8. Valse–Barcarolle

9. Cakewalk

10. Recitative

11. Iberia

12. Monkey Nuts

13. Cabana

14. Green Tomatoes

15. On Time

16. Rag-a-muffin

Alan Haughton

Rhythm&Rag
for B flat Saxophone

Contents

1. Prelude *2*
2. Flying High *4*
3. Slow Motion *5*
4. Three's Company *6*
5. Nocturne *8*
6. Blues 9 *10*
7. Fives *11*
8. Valse – Barcarolle *12*
9. Cakewalk *14*
10. Recitative *16*
11. Iberia *18*
12. Monkey Nuts *20*
13. Cabana *22*
14. Green Tomatoes *24*
15. On Time *26*
16. Rag-a-muffin *28*

The Associated Board of
the Royal Schools of Music

for Stephen Davies

Rhythm & Rag for B flat Saxophone

ALAN HAUGHTON

1. Prelude

AB 2752

2. Flying High

3. Slow Motion

4. Three's Company

D. S. al Coda

CODA

8

5. Nocturne

6. Blues 9

7. Fives

12

8. Valse–Barcarolle

9. Cakewalk

10. Recitative

11. Iberia

12. Monkey Nuts

13. Cabana

24

14. Green Tomatoes

15. On Time

16. Rag-a-muffin

Printed in the United Kingdom by
Caligraving Limited, Thetford, Norfolk